Jackson –
May your life
be fill with love
& laughter.
Jean Bennett

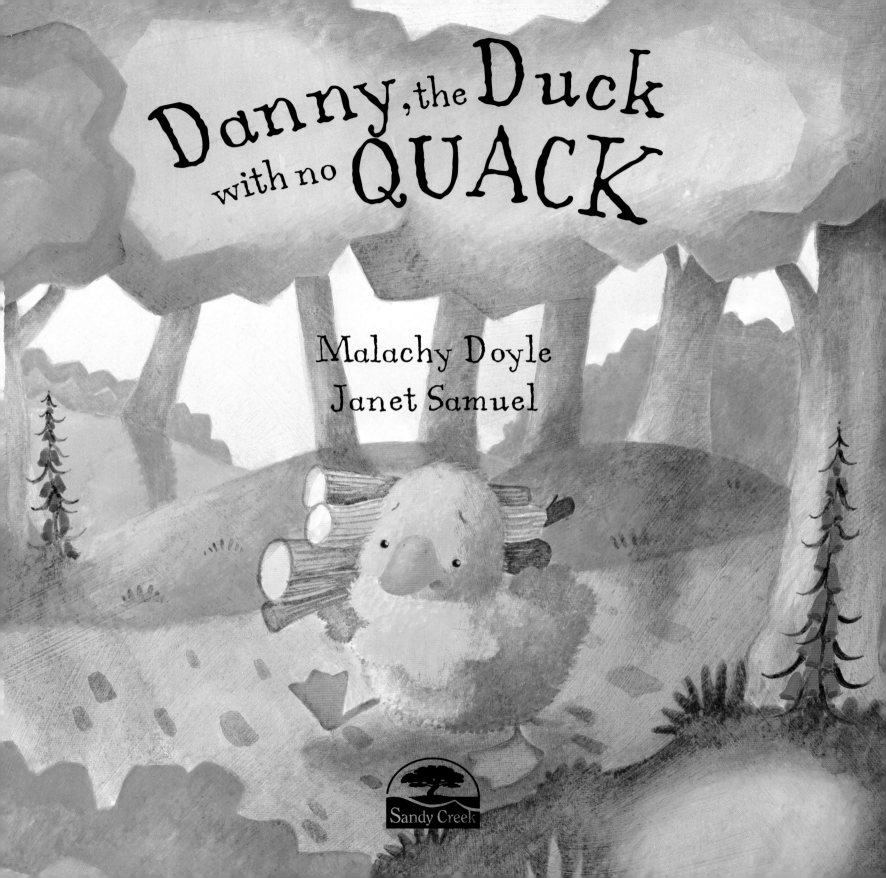

Danny, the Duck with no QUACK

Malachy Doyle
Janet Samuel

Sandy Creek

Every morning, the ducks and the hens gather in the yard for a chat.

"How's the quack, Danny?" asks a chicken. "What's the story? Tell us the news."

But Danny's a shy little duck,
and he never knows what to say.

He keeps his beak
firmly shut, bows his
head, and turns away.

"Come on, Danny!" squawk the birds one day. "Don't be such a scaredy-quack! There must be something you can tell us!"

Danny swallows and opens his beak—but nothing comes out.

Not a peep, not a splutter, not a cackle, not a hoot. He's **lost his quack!**

Right, thinks Danny, that's it.
And he takes off up the lane
to find a tale worth telling.

Yes, he wanders up the track
to find his quack.

He waddles along and waddles along,
till he meets two scrawny foxes.

And Danny knows he shouldn't
—these are tricky-looking foxes.

He opens his beak to say that he won't.
But nothing comes out.

And Danny knows he shouldn't
—these are hungry-looking foxes.
He opens his mouth to say no.

But he can't.

"Now who'll fill the pot with water?"
asks one fox.
"The duck with no quack,"
smirks the other.

And Danny knows he shouldn't —these are scary-looking foxes.

He opens his beak as wide as he can, and what does he say?

Nothing.

"The duck with no quack!" cries the other, jumping up.

They rush toward Danny and they're just about to grab him, when...

He throws himself to
the side of the pot.

The two foxes are so surprised,
they tumble right inside!

"How's the quack, Danny?" ask the other ducks, when he rushes back to the farmyard.
"Yeah, what's the cluck, duck?" ask the hens.

And aren't they all amazed to hear Danny quacking?

Aren't they all astonished at the tale he has to tell?

"Go away!" cluck the angry hens.

"And don't come back!" quack the ducks.

And Danny's quack is the loudest.

"Quackity-quack!" he says.
"Don't come back!"

QUACK!

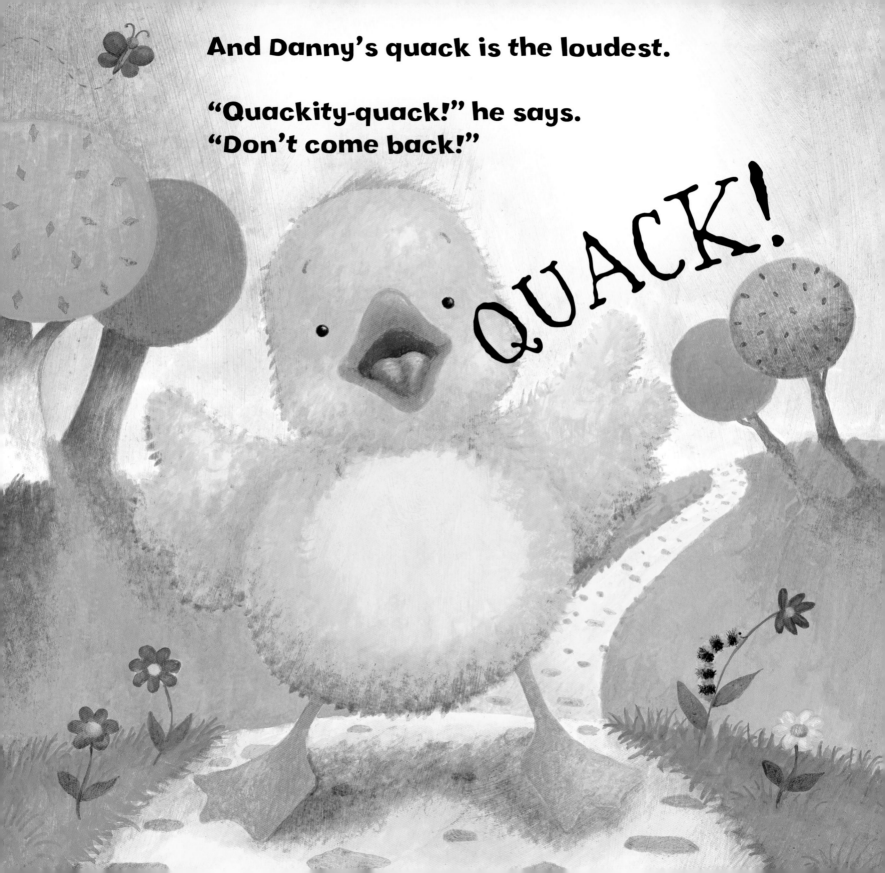

Author Malachy Doyle
Illustrator Janet Samuel
Designer Alix Wood
Project Editor Heather Amery

Publisher Steve Evans
Creative Director Zeta Davies

Sandy Creek
122 Fifth Avenue
New York, NY 10011

ISBN 978 1 4351 2037 2

Library of Congress Cataloging-in-Publication Data

Doyle, Malachy.
 Danny, the duck with no quack / by Malachy Doyle ;
illustrated by Janet Samuel.
     p. cm. -- (QEB storytime)

Summary: Shy little Danny the duck goes in search of his
missing quack, only to find that it takes two tricky foxes to
solve the problem.
 ISBN 978-1-59566-754-0 (hardcover)
[1. Ducks--Fiction. 2. Bashfulness--Fiction. 3. Adventure
and adventurers--Fiction.] I. Samuel, Janet, ill. II. Title.
PZ7.D775Dan 2010
 [E]--dc22
                              2009001994

Printed and bound in China

10 9 8 7 6 5 4 3 2 1